Hopeful Hope

*Perseverance and Education
Is the Answer*

HOPE BALDWIN

Fulton Books
Meadville, PA

Published by Fulton Books 2024

ISBN 979-8-89221-021-8 (paperback)
ISBN 979-8-89221-023-2 (digital)

Printed in the United States of America

Dedication

I dedicate this book to everyone who grew up in Newark, New Jersey, high-rise projects and the surrounding areas in the 1960s and 1970s. We know that the struggle is real. Also, to their children and grandchildren who do not understand where they are coming from amid conversations, music, and disciplinary actions. Congratulations to everyone who are where they want to be in life. No judging.

Introduction

This is a collection of stories of how perseverance and education can result to success. How being optimistic can result in positive actions, causing someone to obtain all their goals. Surrounding yourself with positive and supportive people whom you feel comfortable around make life much easier to endure. Acknowledging and embracing the fact that challenges and adversaries are inevitable. You just need to figure out how to show up.

have been inspired by an African-American young lady, whom I am going to call Hopeful Hope. We grew up in Newark, New Jersey, in the seventies. Our paths had crossed numerous times. We had many conversations regarding our inner-city life experiences. She had inspired me to persevere during many of my adversities. Her creative survival skills have encouraged me to believe that I can achieve my dreams. Her dare to dream that she can achieve her "American dream" was intriguing to me. She always remained hopeful about positive outcomes regarding hopeless situations. She was willing to make many sacrifices to obtain her dream. Hope has exceeded my expectations of the success of someone who has been raised in her environment. I have been encouraged by many people to tell her story. Unlike Hope, I have not earned any degrees. After graduating from high school, I met the love of my life, we were married, and we had three children. We decide to continue to reside in Newark.

Well, here it goes!

Hopeful Hope: The Hood

Hopeful Hope lived in poverty. She lived in one of the most dangerous cities in the state of New Jersey and in the worst area. A place where rapists, murderers, and psychopaths resided and were known by their legal names. They were punished as the neighborhood decided. In most cases, they were not apprehended because they were feared. If a large group of bad people decided to go after them, they would leave town and return in a couple of years. Then they were allowed to continue to live in the neighborhood as a standup citizen, according to their definition. Hopeful Hope lived in a place where there were many deaths in the stairways. The deaths were mostly drug related or regarding illegal money transactions. Daily rapes and robberies occurred in the hallways and the elevators. She lived in a high-crime area where it took a policeman over an hour to respond to a crime. She witnessed high-speed police chases where the children played. The police chases were causing many accidents and fatalities. Police brutality occurred daily, increasing tension in the community. The policemen in the area constantly took the drug dealer's money, and they beat anyone that got in their way. Drug dealers and the gangs controlled most of the area. The drug dealers were encouraging drug deals on children. Politicians were on the take, and no one was overseeing the care for the children.

The children were playing on dangerous grounds with dangerous tools. Rusty tools got discarded into the grass, sidewalks, and parking lots. Children played with whatever they could find on the ground due to lack of finances. Recreational facilities were few, so children made up their own games with the resources they have. The children roofed hop, and some hopped to their deaths. Old soil mattresses and old furniture got discarded in the streets, and children used them to jump and play on. The elevators were some children's hide-and-seek playground. Repairs were few, resulting in some children stepping to their death when running into the elevator. They were playing on the steps with broken rails and chipped stairs, resulting in major accidental injuries. Babies were crawling to the window then to their death because of lack of window guards. There was a small budget for recreation and education.

Education and educational equipment were of poor quality and dated. Some teachers did not have the passion to encourage children just the passion for a paycheck. Children were being spoken to in a negative tone that broke their spirit and confidence. Some questions were never answered, and some answers were "Because I said so," which did not prevent negative repetitiveness. Slain language rarely got corrected, and reading rarely got encouraged. Children's self-esteem had a slow growth. Lack of personal hygiene got ignored. The children did not get lessons on the values of animals, or how to maintain their neighborhood. Animals were viewed as target practice, kick bags, and sometimes were thrown off the roof like flying saucers. Riots broke out downtown Newark and Springfield Avenue because the children were not being taught how to articulate what they view as unfair treatment. Care for the neighborhood never seemed to come up in conversations. Some schools have difficulty getting teachers, so substitutes and unqualified persons were given teaching jobs. Tenants from the neighborhood who were familiar with the children and their families were likely to become the teachers and administration personnel.

Some tenants refused to attempt any repairs in their apartments. They would wait days, months, and sometimes years for housing authorities to send a repairman. They have low-income rent apartments and refused to perform any upkeep inside or outside the apartments. They were leaving debris in the hallways and sidewalks. The apartments get enough heat to fry eggs in the winter. The tenants open the windows for comfort. That is one repair that never got fixed. The apartments were either too cold or too hot, and most tenants rather it be too hot because adjusting the heat was a simple process. The apartments didn't have a thermostat for control. All they have to do was crack a couple of windows. So complaints about the apartments being too hot rarely got submitted. Adjusting the cold means purchasing a heater, which could cause a fire or accidental burns. The cold could cause discomfort and illness with children and elderly people. Adjusting the heat was a no-brainer and had become the normal living conditions in the hood. Plus, expecting some custodians to do work was a bad joke. Some of them were on drugs and never worked. The ones that did work got challenged with the working tools. Some custodians were using the tools and cleaning supplies purchased to clean the buildings for personal use. Some solutions were low quality, and some do not clean because the custodians added water to compensate for their stealing. Too much water diluted the solution, and when they were cleaning, nothing got clean, causing the tenants to continue to live in filthy buildings.

Upon entering a building, a child might witness a sexual act, a robbery in progress, people doing drugs, people dancing to loud music, gambling, and someone relieving themselves. Some might see a human or animal corps. Graffiti is everywhere—inside and outside the buildings, on the walls, on the sidewalks, on the steps, inside the elevators, and on the poles. Some people marked their turf and wrote on the entry door to their apartments. Some people put their names and warning signs to present fear. There were numerous gestures and writings all over the place. No one attempted to clean it up anymore because it had become yet another normal living condition in the hood. Some children were constantly looking for an escape. Everyone's definition of an escape had a different meaning. Some escaped by selling their bodies, selling drugs, or mating with an older person who could financially support them. And some tried to escape the right way.

Hopeful Hope is the ninth child by her mother and the fifth child by her father, that she knew. She had met all her siblings and most of her stepmothers. She enjoyed having a large family. Although watching her mother struggle to feed everyone and attend to everyone's needs was no joy for her. She attempted to assist her mother in any way that she could. She got good grades in school so her mother do not have to stress over her. Her siblings gave her enough reasons to stress about. They did not succeed in getting good grades. She was not sure if it was on purpose, for lack of trying, or if they were academically challenged. They rather enjoy life in their own rights. She did extra chores so her mother do not have to come home to an untidy house. Her siblings did their chores at their leisure, although they knew it would upset their mother. She also assisted her mom with cooking on most Sundays. She enjoyed spending time with her mom, and cooking did not seem like work. Plus, she enjoyed learning how to cook soul food. She enjoyed eating soul food and would like to not have to wait for someone to cook it for her. She was always looking for ways to impress her mother because she loved to see her smile. She thought her mother endured many sad days, and making her smile brightened up her day. Trying to put a smile on her mom's face encouraged Hopeful Hope to do well in school and did all her chores without being told. Sometimes Hope did her siblings' chores to prevent her mom from getting upset.

Hope's mother, Mary, is very active in the community. She is a positive figure and influences many people regarding persevering toward a positive mindset. She is well respected and enjoys helping people in need. She is visible at the elementary school, is a member of the PTA, and she worked closely with the Housing Authority employees. She was aware of all the housing authority's processes, and she had many "go-to" people when she needed to ensure a positive outcome. Mary constantly tried to assist young families and people in an overcrowded apartment by getting the qualified adults an apartment in the Newark Housing Authority. When young families were in jeopardy of being homeless, Mary went out of her way to push their application through the system. She was constantly contacting elected officials to attempt to ensure better living conditions and food programs in the projects. She also encouraged everyone to volunteer with the children's recreational programs. Her most passionate concerns were the care of the children's health and welfare. She corrected everyone's bad language and disrespectful behaviors. She was a mother figure to everyone in the neighborhood and got respected as such. Mary loved to dance and listen to music. It doesn't matter if the song was fast or slow, she would dance often when she heard music. Her mom was the daughter of two college professors who also loved music. Her mom played the piano as she hummed along. She had ten siblings, and they were a very close family. They did many things together, like shopping, attending social events, attending each other's celebrations and their children's celebrations. Once a month or so, they would meet at a neighborhood bar called Peoples Tavern on Van Vechten Street and socialize. They were constantly conversing on the phone about their life-changing experiences, changes in their children's lives, and their grandchildren's lives. Sometimes, their conversations turned into gossip about their neighbors' lives and the community's crimes. They authentically enjoyed each other's company. She came from a huge family, and everyone loved music. It was impossible to remember everyone's name and birthday. There were plenty of good times and plenty of bad times.

There were many nights when they were short on food and extra on disagreements. Many nights plenty of things were not in their rightful place. Lots of disrespect toward one another that laugher and love followed. Gambling was the family's favorite pastime. They loved to play Po Ke No, Bingo, Spades, and Pitty Pat. Gambling always presented the calm before the storm. There were lots of smiles, laughter, and happy talks while gambling. Hopeful Hope is not a gambler, but she loved to watch and enjoyed the happiness it brought. Listening to her siblings reminisce about the past allowed her to get to know her family's tree and her family's ties. Her family loved to socialize. Many people in the neighborhood frequented her family's house because they knew there were always good company and delicious food available. It didn't matter who was home. They were all great listeners who were eager to laugh. There were always a cookout, a birthday celebration, or an appreciation party going on. All the celebrations encouraged Hopeful Hope's cooking skills, and she became more acquainted with her relatives.

Hopeful Hope loved dressing up in high heels and wearing the latest fashions. She took pride in maintaining her girly figure and her neat hairstyles. Makeup and wigs were not something she could wear during the summer months. Hot weather was not her favorite weather. She loved cool weather and snowy days. She jogged and walked in Weequahic Park with whoever wanted to join her. She was constantly attempting to get family and friends to join her, although she preferred to walk alone. Walking alone gave her time to think and plan her day. It also allowed her to process situations she didn't understand. She is a high achiever, with great ideas. She is outspoken but shy around people she is attempting to impress. She loves to laugh and socialize with family members and close friends. She doesn't talk to strangers much but would allow people to grow on her in her own time. Forced relationships would force her to put her guard up for a massive amount of time. Dancing, listening to music, and exercising were her favorite pastimes. When she's not able to exercise, she listened to music. Listening to music also encouraged her life-planning strategies.

Hopeful Hope had dreams of being a lawyer or a journalist. She loved a good debate and revealing researched information. She watched the news and imagined herself being a news broadcaster. Sometimes she stood in front of the mirror and practiced telling the news. She had concerns about her parents' ability to pay for college, so she was constantly considering alternate routes to escape her life of poverty. She was always hoping for greater things, like better living conditions and better finances. She constantly dreamed about someone giving her money and giving her a big house to live in and giving her a fancy car. She also dreamed about winning contests that offers huge monetary rewards. She watched television shows like *The Price Is Right* and *The Wheel of Fortune* and had dreams of being the winner. She had thoughts about earning money to buy those things, but it seemed like it would take a long time to acquire and too much hard work, and it might take away a lot of her fun time. So she began to think of fun ways to make money so she didn't have to stop having fun and to enjoy financial success. Hopeful Hope started babysitting because she loved kids, and she had fun hanging out with them. She began braiding their hair because she enjoyed braiding hair. While she was earning money braiding hair, she was also making money babysitting the children. Hopeful Hope was becoming very hopeful about her financial success that did not require higher education and hard work. She was excited about having fun while earning money. Hopeful Hope's great idea was now being imitated by many of her neighbors, and business began to slow down. Hopeful Hope reinvented herself by offering to take children to and from camp, in addition to staying overnight at her neighborhood's house in the summer and during weekends. Again, many of the neighborhood children began to imitate her idea, and business began to slow up. Again, Hopeful Hope reinvented herself and started selling cake and lemonade outside her apartment building, but that could only be done during the summer months. Plus, most people would only support the sell if the profits were being donated toward organizations who supported recreational projects for the neighborhood children. Hopeful Hope began to get discouraged and began being a child again. She joined the neighborhood drill team called the Shondells and the Girl Scout. Then she began playing kickball more and attending summer camps and learned how to fish. Life is fun being a child. She was a very active child and enjoyed keeping busy. She decided to leave all her financial worries to her parents.

Hopeful Hope was now twelve years old, and it was 1979. She was working odd jobs to prevent working hard and seeking higher education. She was working in her father's store some weekends, going to the store for neighbors, and babysitting for family members. She thrived for better living conditions and finances. Hopeful Hope kept all her monies in a jewelry box on her dresser in her bedroom. Her plan was to buy a bike one day. She thought it would be a fun exercise, and it might be beneficial when running errands. One day, she sadly realized that not only was her money missing, but so was the jewelry box. Hopeful Hope now had feelings of hopelessness. She worked so hard for that money that she was constantly reinventing herself as she remained hopeful for a great financial future with no hard work. Now she had to start all over again. Hopeful Hope decided to give up on great success and finance and settled for the poverty life she was born into. She began to focus on school assignments, school activities, and neighborhood functions.

Graduation from Dayton St. Elementary School was approaching, and she needed to focus on her attire and celebration plans. After graduation, she met up with a couple of friends and took the train to New York. When they got to "the Big Apple," they began to walk around as they told jokes and enjoyed the sites of the city. They decided to make a stop and got something to eat. More laughs and jokes about "hood" life. They began to make plans of better future living, escaping the "hood" life, and raising their children in a house that is in a better community. They joked about dressing their children in nice clothes and always having food in their house as they compared their lives in the hood. They constantly recognized and appreciated how their parents did the best they could with their resources. But it always got announced how better decisions was an option for their parents, and many options were not always being taken advantage. Hopeful Hope enjoyed hanging out with her childhood friends and laughing about old times. Soon, they would be attending high school and might never get a chance to hang out together in New York again. Who knows how their schedules would be or how their mind-sets would evolve or what road their personal growth would take them. They were enjoying what might be their last days together as children of the hood. The completion of high school would definitely change them. Hopeful Hope decided to cut her hair short and lose a couple of pounds as she entered into the beginning of her adulthood. She already had a slim figure, but she wanted to be sexy slim.

Graduating from elementary school is a scary process because she considered it to be the first step into adulthood. Most children in her neighborhood did not graduate from high school. The children that started were made to believe that it was such a hard social process, and the constant testing was embar-rassing for the failures. Doing homework at home in a stressful environment was a difficult process. It was also difficult to concentrate when you are hungry and have nothing to eat. It was also hard to concen-trate when there were many violent acts going on in the neighborhood and constantly conflicting discus-sions inside the household, although a small percent-age of the children from her neighborhood managed to become successful in their own right.

Hopeful Hope managed to earn acceptance to one of the most scholastic high schools in Newark. Acceptance to Science High School requires a test and an essay. They also considered the applicant's elementary school grades. She was so excited and nervous at the same time. Her mother and father were so proud of her. They always bragged about how they knew Hope would make it out of the hood because they saw her determination. She was constantly discussing her future plans with them and shared her thoughts regarding their living conditions. There was no doubt in their minds that she will get her acceptance to whatever school she applied to. Her acceptance had increased her self-esteem. She had heard about the college financial aid plan for low-income students and now she had hopes of being a lawyer or a journalist again. Completing college had become one of her life goals again. She was willing to work hard and put the work in if her schooling do not cause financial pressure for her parents. She rather they save their worries for her siblings. They paid little attention to her because she seemed to have it all together.

Hopeful Hope got a summer job to purchase her school clothes. She loved to dress up and color coordinate her clothes. A week before school began, she woke up on a Saturday morning to find that her school clothes went missing out of her bedroom closet by a close family member. Again, Hopeful Hope began to feel hopeless. She could not afford any new clothes. Everyone in the household were arguing and placing blame until it was found out that a close relative had taken them. Someone that did not live in the house but resided in the neighborhood. Hopeful Hope was so disappointed. She thinks that was a very selfish and inconsiderate act. The relative was in constant denial and refused to apologize. Some of the clothes were sold, and some were given to a friend. Hopeful Hope decided to go visit her father. He has a way of making her appreciate her life's lessons. She caught two buses to cry on her father's shoulder. He called Hope's relative a bum as he explained how some people would never work and would always prey on other people's property. Hope's father gave her money to replace some of her school clothes and advised her to purchase a trunk with a lock. Hope's father constantly reminded her how she doesn't fit in the project lifestyle.

He said, "Baby girl, you are like a rose in a garden of weeds." She never understood her father's old-school talks but enjoyed his company tremendously.

Hope said, "Daddy, I can't wait to get out of there."

Her dad said, "Well, school is the answer, baby girl. You have to put the work in. You have to stop daydreaming and staring out of the window because that will not cut it."

He made her feel safe and at home. Hope visited her father often. He was her escape from the hood. He had escaped from the poverty life he was born into. She loved to hear his stories of his struggles and triumphs. He is no millionaire, but he managed to live in the comforts he so desire. He always advised her that education is the key to all successes.

Her father, Thurman, is a recovering alcoholic. Soon after kicking alcohol, he got diagnosed with emphysema. He continued to smoke cigarettes and drink coffee daily against the advice of his doctor. He was not a big eater and spent long hours working at maintaining his business. Hopeful Hope suggested he get someone to manage his business, and he laughed. He said he do not know anyone that he could trust. He used to trust everyone and was constantly given reasons not to trust others. Then one day, he stopped trusting everyone. He did not put his money in the bank. He rather kept it under his mattress and in garbage bags.

He is what Hope calls "an old school and an old G." It was consistent with the lifestyle he grew up in. Every time Hope visited her father, his cough seemed to be getting worse. She did not worry about him much because his main girlfriend is a nurse. She was aware of all his side chicks. She spent a lot of time caring for Thurman and very little time caring for herself. She was aware of all his symptoms and medicine dosages. Taking care of Thurman had to be a challenge because of all his extracurricular activities. Hope constantly wondered if she loved him or if she stayed around to prevent others from getting him. She was very pleasant, but she could not hide her pain. It was all over her face, especially when she thinks no one is looking. Hope is very observant. She was constantly being attentive to people's body language. Her main stepmother's smiles and laughs seemed to be a struggle as she interacted with Hope and her siblings. Thurman is a small man. He weighs approximately one hundred pounds and wears his hair long. Hope was constantly trying to get him to put his hair in a ponytail and allow her to braid it.

He looked at her in disgust and said, "Girl, get away from me."

Then he joked and continued, "Real men don't wear their hair like that," as he shook his head and smiled.

He wore a suit and hat every day as he maintained his business. His business consisted of a neighborhood bar, a laundry, and a convenient store. Hope had never seen her father in jeans, sneakers, sweat socks, or sandals. He owned multiple businesses and constantly dressed in professional clothes even when he was attending to the business at the laundry. On Father's Day, Hope decided to purchase her father a pair of jeans. She was excited about her selection because she knew he did not have any jeans. She took advantage of the opportunity to check his closet when she was at his house. On Father's Day, she presented the gift, a pair of jeans, hand-wrapped in a box. She insisted he open the box in front of her. Her father opened the box and began to laugh. Hope looked at him in confusion.

She asked him, "Dad, why are you laughing?"

He said, "Have you ever seen me wear jeans?"

Hope replied, "No, Dad, that's why I bought you a pair."

He said, "That's because I don't wear jeans because I don't like the way it looks on me." Then he joked, "Real men don't wear jeans."

Hope assumed that there was more to that joke but refused to get deep into it. She never seemed to get his jokes, but his laugh was contagious. He is a serious man and doesn't laugh much. Plus, she loves to see him smile. It is much better than to see him stressed about business or her brother. So she began to laugh also. Her father gave her a big hug and kiss on the cheek as he thanked her for the jeans. He then handed her the jeans back and insisted that she takes them back and get her a pair of jeans. She was so excited about how she made her father laugh and gave him a reason to give her a hug and a kiss. Her father is not an affectionate person, and his affection brought tears to her eyes. After leaving her father's store, Hope went straight to Bamberger's basement, downtown Newark, and exchanged the Calvin Klein's jeans to her size. She enjoyed wearing new clothes. Hope is the ninth child and rarely receives new clothes. Most of her clothes were "hand-me-downs" from her sisters. Hope and her sisters did not share the same taste in clothes, so Hope never appreciated her "hand-me-down" outfits. She considered herself a more conservative but fashionable dresser. She only liked clothes that were more than likely to not go out of style, and that only included certain prints. It also excluded clothes with any type of bling (shiny or glitter) on it. Hopeful Hope enjoyed color coordinating her clothes with her accessories. She decided to save her new jeans for the first day of high school.

High school began in a couple of days, and Hope was well prepared. She had her school supplies, school clothes, her new hairdo, her bus card, and her high heels. She was constantly planning her schedule and considered what school activities she will join to begin building her college resume. She was told by one of her newfound family members at Newark City Hall that colleges consider applicants high school grades and activities when considering applications. Her high school did not have a sports program. It was connected with Central High School, which was a couple of blocks from Science High School. Central High School is known for its violence. Hope was unsure if she wanted to subject herself back into that environment again. Most of the children that attended Science High School were from the best neighborhoods in the city of Newark and the most academic children from the projects. Science High School has an impressive graduation rate, and most of the graduates attended college or a technical school—children with plans to improve their living condition, increase their personal growth, and make their mark in society. Children that are respectful and consider other people's positions. They were not as rough around the edges as most people were in the projects. Most of the students in Science High School were considered to be soft (less likely to fight) or the cream of the crop in their neighborhood. Fighting was not their end results to negative approaches, and an apology was an easy response for them. They were friendly debaters and people that would walk away from situations that were not debatable. She was familiar with the violent people from her neighborhood. She believed being around violent people she did not know was not a good idea. There would always be a test even if it was not agreed upon or warranted by the others in the group. I guessed it was considered the test of time. Some people in the hood liked to know who was entering their domain. They needed to know if they could trust the person they were interacting with, if that person would have their back, or if that person was worth being allowed to maneuverer around their comfort zone.

Sometimes the test might consist of someone playing a joke, borrowing money and not paying it back (just to see your reaction), or offering a wrestling or boxing competition. Sometimes the test turned into a real fight, which might be the real test. They might want to see if they could beat someone if they wanted or needed to. After thinking about it for weeks and considering many aspects of the probabilities, Hope decided she would just focus on her class assignments and get to know everyone and how everyone rolls before joining any outside activities. She had already decided to join the band. Science High School had a band. She already made a promise to her eighth-grade teacher, Mrs. Barnes, that she would join the band. Mrs. Barnes brother was the music teaches, and he was also the band instructor. Her instrument of choice was a clarinet. She was hoping to meet new friends and learn new ways of going about life. The people she resided around went about things in similar ways. When she listened to adult conversations, she realized that everyone was in agreement with the ways each other's disciplined their children, cooked their food, went about paying their bills, and the ways each other went about their relationships. They were all raised the same way by a group of people who had lived in very similar ways. Hope wanted to break the cycle, and her first move would involve moving out of the neighborhood. She would always continue to frequent close friends, but Hope needed different! She needed to learn how things could be handle differently and more efficiently. She was aware that the transition would not change overnight, but she wanted to gain a mindset to be open for positive lessons. She wanted to learn how to think differently. She wanted to be viewed as a person that was willing to be open for change and inspire to break her family's cycle—the cycle of incomplete education, the cycle of teenage pregnancy, and the cycle of not knowing when to end the party. Joining activities at Central High School and subjecting herself around the same lifestyles was a no-brainer. She needed to escape. Being around unencouraged people would not encourage her in succeeding her goal to increase her personal growth and learning how to think differently.

Hopeful Hope: Perseverance

ope now knew she must change her mindset. She must cease being hopeful and begin putting in the work to make her financial success happen. She knew she could remain hopeful, but it must be collaborated with collective hard work and less fun. She was aware that making money might not be fun, and higher education was essential to her personal growth.

The first day of high school, Hope was very nervous. She used to be one of the most intelligent student in all her classes in elementary school. Now she would be in classes where all the students were one of the most intelligent students in their classes in elementary school. She did not know anyone, and she felt overdressed. Dressing down made her feel down, so she constantly dressed in business attire. She dressed in high heels, suits, and jackets. She had feelings of being alone. Most of her neighborhood friends went to Malcolm X Shabazz High School, and she had been accepted to Science High School. She caught the same bus as her neighborhood friends, but their destination came before hers. Hope always went to school early to avoid any possibility of tardiness and so she never sees any of her neighborhood friends at the bus stop. High school was the beginning of Hope's distancing herself from her neighborhood. She believed her personal growth might be a struggle in the hood. She wanted to surround herself around positive and inspirational people. People she could learn from and collaborate with about great possibilities. Thoughts about leaving her neighborhood was very scary for her because it was her comfort zone. She had never been introduced to life outside her neighborhood. She knew she was heading in the right direction but that did not prevented her from wanting to crawl into her closet with a television. She wanted to stay in her closet until a miracle happens in her favor. She had been on trips outside New Jersey but never long enough to witness other cultural ways of living. Television was the closest she had been to knowing other cultural ways of living. Most of the shows she watched were fiction. There were other ethnicities who resided in her neighborhood, but it appeared their cultural lifestyles were very similar to hers. She was not sure if it was a poverty thing, or if their cultures were similar. She was not sure if educated people and people of wealth lived differently because they can afford to.

Her first day of school, she entered the class and saw her classmates in their new clothes and fresh hairstyles. They all seemed so excited to be in class. She was so used to people dreading school and cutting classes every chance they get. It was so refreshing for her to be surrounded with people that enjoyed school like she did. Everyone was talking and laughing and checking each other out. They were not complaining about missed meals, family disputes, and missing items. Hope overheard some conversations and began to laugh. Her laughter caught a couple of student's attention, and they began to laugh also. She was not sure if they heard what she heard or if they were laughing at her laugh. People began telling their jokes and funny stories near Hope because they liked to hear her laugh. Hope is very social and enjoys listening to a good joke and a funny story. She laughs at funny stories all day in school, catching the attention of all the class clowns. Each class she attended, the class clown constantly kept an eye on her. She was a happy person and enjoyed being inspired to enjoy life by sharing a funny story or a good joke.

It was now the third week of school, and she began meeting more people and their friends. She was getting compliments on her wardrobe and her neat hairdos. High school was now a great place for her. She no longer felt alone or scared or overdressed. After a couple of months in high school, Hope felt very popular. Everyone was speaking to her, and she was enjoying high school. She continued to persevere in high school by doing her homework and passing her classes. The other students were very helpful there were no competitions or unwarranted tension. Hope enjoyed school.

Her mom's asked her, "Hope, how is school?"

She told her mother, "We are one happy family trying to get our high school diploma." It was a great escape from the hood for her.

She continued to see some of her neighborhood friends in passing. Nakeedah was one of Hope's neighborhood friend.

Nakeedah asked, "Hey, girl, where have you been?"

Hope responded, "I have been inside doing my homework."

Nakeedah said, "Yeah, girl, I heard that school gives a lot of homework. I am glad I don't go there."

Hope smiled and continued to walk away as she thought to herself, *Well, I am glad that I do because I am getting the hell out of the hood*. She began to hang around the neighborhood less and less. She began to feel like an outsider in the very neighborhood she was raised in because none of her friends talked about college or improving their living conditions. She heard many talks about the new name brand outfits they brought or will buy or want to buy. She heard conversation about the new hairstyles they were getting and the movies they had watched or will watch at the movies theater. The useless conversations were never-ending. Hope wished to be in the position to enjoy all those things, but first, she would rather complete school and earn a degree. She kept thinking that she must stay focus and keep things in perspective. She was aware that they were only fourteen and fifteen years old, but it was the conversation she needed to feel inspired. She knew how people in the neighborhood were quick to accuse someone of thinking they were better than others or thinks people forget where they came from. So she did not feel comfortable speaking about her college plans.

She met a couple a friends at school who were from similar backgrounds. They laughed at the same jokes as Hope and have similar concerns. Two were raised in the projects like Hope, in a single-parent household, and two were raised in a two-parent household. All their struggles were similar—living in a dangerous neighborhood, part of a large family, endure similar financial worries, and have family members living their lives in ways their parents disapprove of. Hope and her newfound friends spent plenty of time together. They were together during lunchtime, before class, and after school. High school was no longer a place where she gets nervous. She now has friends who made her feel comfortable and was a part of their group. She and her new girlfriends shared many new experiences about school issues, life expectancies, and future plans. Together, they figured out many life lessons and concerns. They helped each other with homework and classwork. They shared their first boyfriend experience and private family conflicts. She managed to stay out of trouble, although her and her girlfriends experienced some conflicting situations.

It was a nice day. Hope and her friends were in the lunchroom. Her girlfriends stopped to chat and Hope got her lunch and went straight to the table to eat because she was hungry. She did not eat dinner the night before. There was no food available last night, so she prepared for school, took a shower, and went to bed. Then there was no breakfast available, so she got dressed and went to school.

This angry girl, Shonda, approached Hope and accused her and her girlfriends of jumping her and her girlfriends at Club Zanzibar on Broad Street. Hope did not attend that party. She had no idea what Shonda was talking about. Her girlfriends did not mention any fight to her. Her friends got into a spat with her friends and badly beat them up before Hope could explain Shonda swung at her then Hope threw her over the table. Her girlfriends and security came running over. The witnesses told security that Hope was defending herself, so she did not get a suspension like Shonda. Security walked Shonda to the main office to process her suspension. Her girlfriends began to laugh, making it hard for Hope to remain upset.

Hope said, "What the hell is she talking about? Who did you guys beat up at the Club Zanzibar last weekend?"

Her girlfriend began laughing louder and harder. They began to tell her that they were flirting with one of Shonda's friend's boyfriend and then before they knew it curses and fists started flying, and they were put out of the club. They were laughing as they revealed their story, and of course, Hope began to laugh as she called them crazy. They told Hope how she missed all the fun.

Three weeks later, they were still talking about how Hope threw Shonda over the table. Hope was not proud of it. She was not exactly sure where her strength came from, but every time they brought it up, she would not say anything because she knew they were having fun reminiscing. Everything happened so fast she was attempting to get an angry person, who was attacking her, as far away from her as possible. She was surprised of her own strength.

Hope and her girlfriends decided to attend one of the basketball games at Central High School. It was a popular game: Central High School versus Malcolm X Shabazz. The games always got many spectators. Hope's girlfriend, Nancy, was attracted to one of the Central High basketball players. As they entered the school building, Chila noticed some girls that her and her cousins had a beef with at Club Khayyam. She began telling the story about how the fight came to blows. As she was telling the story, Hope thought to herself, *OMG! Here we go again.* She immediately began thinking about leaving, but she realized the girls noticed them also. Walking to the 31 bus stop by herself would not be a good idea right now. So she began looking at all the exits and became familiar with her surroundings. Hope and her girlfriends decided to sit in the front row to get Sam's, the basketball player who Nancy was attracted to, attention when he was sitting on the bench. Hope was unable to focus on the game. She was constantly watching the girls Chila and her cousins had a beef with at the club.

Now the game was over, and Nancy wanted to flirt with Sam and Chila noticed one of his friends on the basketball team. As they were chatting and flirting with members of the basketball team, the girls came over to Chila and said, "Now what was all that smack you were talking at the club? I see you don't have your bodyguards with you today."

Hope thought to herself, *Here we go!*

Some members on the basket team intervened, and Hope and her girlfriends began walking toward the bus stop with some members of the basketball team. Hope thought to herself, *Whoosh! That was close.* She decided to never go to another high school basketball game again in Newark. She constantly reminded herself of her mother's words: "You are judged by the company you keep and will be punished as such." Thoughts of discontinuing her girlfriend's friendship never entered her mind. She knew they were defending themselves, and they were not going around starting fights. Although flirting with other people's boyfriends did not help matters any. They were in the hood and appeared weak and might cause people to challenge them more than usual.

It was a nice day outside, and Hope and her girlfriends were now leaving school, walking toward the bus stop on Broad and Market. They walked the same path every day. As they were walking, Chila noticed Shonda was there and was looking in their direction. Hope decided to ignore her because she didn't want any trouble. As they approached the bus stop, her girlfriend, Chile, immediately began arguing with her. Shonda pulled out a knife on Broad Street, in front of Dunkin Donut. Everyone at the bus stop began to back up as they continued to look on, except Hope and her girlfriends. They continued to walk toward Shonda. Then Chila pulled out a gun as she continued to argue. Hope's legs became weak, but she managed to continue to stand. There were talk around town that Shonda was going to retaliate by bringing a gun or a knife to school. Chila decided to protect herself by traveling with a gun—a gun she borrowed from her father without his permission. She neglected to share her concerns with her friends. For a second, Hope felt like she was back in the hood. Without thinking, Hope punched Shonda in the face, and she dropped her knife and immediately picked it up then started running down Broad Street, toward Market Street. Hope noticed the police and immediately told Chila, "Put that damn gun away." Hope couldn't believe what just happened. They started walking down the street, passing the police car that was driving by. Usually they would hang around downtown on Broad Street and Market and look in some store windows at clothes and shoes they couldn't afford or chat with familiar people. Hope was so disturbed with everyone's actions, including her own. She got on the next 24 City Line bus and went straight home. She now wanted to crawl in a closet and watch television. That was her safe haven. Fortunately, for Hope, it was now Friday, and she had the weekend to recoup.

The time was seven o'clock, and Hope's mother called her to the kitchen to answer a phone call. It was her friend, Chila, who invited her to attend a party at the Peppermint Lounge in East Orange with them. Hope thought to herself, *Is she really serious?*

She responded, "Girl, I am so tired, I have on my PJs, and I am in bed watching televisions."

Hope discovered her limitations early in life. She was aware that her girlfriend's enemies were hers also. Her gut told her to not attend that party. It might not end well for her. She listened to her gut and didn't attend the party.

It was Monday in school, and Chila and her girlfriends were laughing about another fight they had at the Peppermint Lounge Friday night. Again, they said, "Hope, you missed all the fun."

Hope thought to herself, *Are they freaking kidding me right now?*

With all the conflicts surrounding Hope and her girlfriends, she decided to not join any sports activities. She knew that not attending parties did not exonerate her from being attacked. Her and her friends were being considered as one. She knew she could not control what they do, but she had the ability to control her own actions. Hope learned a valuable lesson of choosing her friends. As her mother used to say, "You are judged by the company you keep and will be punished as such," which is one of the reason why she gained a desire to stop hanging around the hood. Hope also knew there was no way to escape conflict completely if she lives in Newark.

She felt blessed with her high school friends because she knew they would always have her back. Friends like them are hard to come by.

She constantly reminded herself how her success in high school was the beginning of her escape out of the hood. She kept an open mind when her girlfriends decided to attend certain parties and social events. If she thought it may be trouble, or if people who they had a beef with may attend, she would not go. The streets talked, and some people gave parties that were known for its conflicts and gun battles. All that information was put on front street. Hope tried to stay away from their parties. Staying focused became more of a challenge, but she managed to persevere.

Hope and her girlfriends met in the morning at the same place when they were at school. Today, her girlfriends were not there. She thought it was very strange for all her girlfriends to be absent at the same time. She went to her locker room to put her jacket, umbrella, and afternoon class books in the locker. Her locker room was on one side of the building, and her girlfriends' locker rooms were on the other side, in the basement. She was not sure if they requested it, or if it was assigned to them. They always met outside the school building, so she never considered asking them. Hope went to their locker room to see if they were in school. As she walked toward their locker room, she began to get upset. She was now wondering if they decided to cut school without offering her an option to go. There was nothing special going on in school today. There was no special test or special assignment due or any class trip planned. She would had enjoyed cutting school today. She got to the doorway of the locker room and began to smell marijuana. Then she began to hear people laughing as she recognized one of her girlfriend's voice. They were hanging out with a couple of guys, and someone was smoking marijuana. She said, "Hey," to her girlfriends. They quickly spoke and returned back to their conversation with their friends. Hope did not want to stay too long in fear of getting the smell in her clothes. She faced one of her girlfriends and said, "Girl, I do not want to be late for class. I will catch up with y'all later." Hope's other fear was a teacher, or an administrator, coming in the basement and suspending everyone without asking any questions. She refused to get blamed for something she did not indulged in. Hope would drink alcohol, but smoking marijuana was not her thing.

Today, she went to school, and her girlfriends were there, and they were smiling and began rushing toward her. One of her girlfriend said, "We have been waiting for you," turned around, and continued, "We are out of here."

This was the day they decided to cut school. Hope was excited to be given an option. She loved options. As she was turning around, Hope did a quick mental scan of her classes and computed that she did not have anything important going on today, no test, special assignments, or a class trip; and with a smile, she turned completely around. They headed down Rector Street, laughing and chatting about how they could not take school today. Everyone has a story why school was not where they wanted to be today. Hope was just going along for the ride. She had no issues about going to school today. Anything beats staying home listening to her mother complain about the actions of her siblings.

Hope had been going to school and working in the summer to buy school clothes for the next school year. She had not been hanging around the neighborhood much. She had been going places with her Science High School girlfriends and hanging out with them around their neighborhood. They all lived in Newark, but Hope's neighborhood was the most dangerous one. She enjoyed meeting new people and learning their ways of living. She was always willing to learn new ideas and different concepts regarding succeeding in life.

It was now Hope's senior year. She began looking back and appreciated her perseverance. She passed all her classes. She was never made to attend summer school to make up for any failed class, although she had come close once. Algebra was not her favorite subject, but with a special teacher who taught algebra one and two and a little help from friends, she managed to pass. Attending Science High School meant attending two science classes daily. People used to see Hope and her girlfriends at the bus stop and would jokingly say, "You are the people that are going to blow up the world," after being made aware of the high school they attended. She enjoyed learning science and watching science-related shows. MacGyver was one of her favorite television shows. The science classes focused a lot on chemicals and the results of mixing them. The assignments were collective and collaborative, which made it fun. Hope enjoyed group work and working with people. Trying to remember all the chemicals and abbreviations presented a challenge for her. Every year, there were more chemicals to remember and the results of some mixtures. She also had to remember which chemicals not to mix. She and her classmates were very careful with the chemicals. There were never any accidents in any of her classes.

Senior year was another terrifying time in Hope's life. Hope would be eighteen years old soon, and that was definitely considered adulthood in her neighborhood. She knew she would be expected to take care of herself. She used to hear adult conversations in her neighborhood regarding how they had been taking care of themselves since they were ten and eleven years old. So she was aware of her possible expectations. Most parents that live in a controlled rent apartment expected their children who did not get good grades in school and have no college plans to get a job and help out with the bills once they turn eighteen. Some other parents that lived in a controlled rent apartments expected their children with college plans to move out and live on campus. She was constantly anticipating her years in college. She was fortunate to have parents that would support her in college. Although they could only stretch their money so far. They have personal bills, Hope's siblings, and their grandchildren to care for. Hope had always been a proactive planner that she shared with her parents. They always expressed their confidence in her success in life and in becoming a stand-up citizen. She would be responsible for her own meals, personal items, and the handling of her college business matters. She had been aware of financial aid for a while and was aware it would provide her with a meal plan and employment. She had been made aware of the availability of counselors and tutors, which made her feel confident in her success in earning her bachelor degree. She anticipated meeting new friends and the love of her life. She spent many hours looking out of her bedroom window daydreaming about her adult life. Sometimes she wished she could turn back the hands of the clock and get some do-overs.

Being a child with no adult concerns were exciting and carefree living. She reminisced about how she used to wake up in the morning without any cares of the world. She would leave all her worries to the adults. Now she was an adult, and all her worries were her own. She used to prepare for her day according to the day of the week. If it was a school day, she would go to school and attend her classes. Then went home and did her homework and her chores. If it was the weekend, she would sleep in, then do her chores and any homework or book report. Once that was done, she would spend some quality time with her mother. They would have a chat to see if her mother needed her to run any errands. Then Hope would reach out to her friends to see where they would be hanging for the weekend. If it was considered a safe place, Hope would gladly hang out with them; if not, she would stay inside and watch television.

It was now senior year, and Hope was mentally preparing for her future challenges.

Senior year seemed to present Hope with many challenges. She now has a boyfriend, pressures of attending college out of state, and her father's health seemed to be deteriorating rapidly. Maintaining her focus was proving to be more of a challenge than she had imagined. She decided to go to college in state because of her father's illness. He was one of her best friends, and she enjoyed his company tremendously. He enjoyed telling her stories because he knew she had a great sense of humor. Sometimes they would talk and laugh for hours. He also grew up in the ghetto, and he enjoyed making jokes about his neighborhood, his family, and old friends. With all her triumphs at home, in school, and after school, she managed to graduate from an academic high school. She decided to try going to college, but she had concerns regarding being able to focus because of lack of finances. Although she qualified for financial aid pocket money, personal items was also a concern. She did not feel confident in working and going to college full-time during her first year. She wanted to focus on class and get familiar with her new environment during her freshman year. Relieving many of her concerns, her and a couple of her high school girlfriends decided to apply for the same college. That was the most encouraging news she had received all year. Knowing they would be there to help her figure out her concerns would lessen her concerns and make it easy to focus on class assignments. Knowing that they would be there made venturing on to the next phase in her life more powerful. She got excited when all of them got their acceptance letters. Her girlfriends decided to begin the summer semester after their high school graduation, and Hope took a summer job at Newark City Hall so she could buy school clothes and supplies.

Newark City Hall was a great place to work. Hope was meeting many influential and successful people in Newark. Everyone went to work with suits and ties, looking very professional. Hope always had been into fashion and any reason to dress up excites her. She learned how to operate many machines and learned the business attire of the working world. She also learned the value of success and the joy of personal growth. Many of the adults at Newark City Hall took her to the side and spoke to her regarding the importance of school and birth control. She had talks about the values of saving money and passing on learned lesson to people with similar backgrounds.

Hope got her first check and decided to open a bank account as advised by one of the employees at Newark City Hall. She had been advised of the expectations and was ready to be an owner of a bank account. She went to Fleet Bank on Broad Street because it was right across the street from Newark City Hall. It was also one bus away from the projects. She could take the 24 bus from her home to the bank. It was also a walk away from the projects. Hope is a walker who could walk long distance. If she did not have bus fare, she could walk to the bank. She liked the fact that it was close to her job. She could cash her check and make deposits on her lunch hour. Taking her check home offered too many chances of it getting lost or coming up missing. The process took longer than she had planned. Now the process was over, and she looked at her bankbook and tears rolled down her cheeks. Getting a bank account was the first part of her success. Before opening the bank account, she made decisions on the amount of her check she would deposit and the amount she would spend on clothes and accessories. Hope took her plans very seriously because living in the hood is unacceptable. Also dating someone from the hood is unacceptable. She thinks if she dated someone from the hood, she would forever live there. Her father constantly reinforced those thoughts to her. Some of them shared their success story and how they persevered to obtaining their position at Newark City Hall. Hope thought getting a job there was a big to-do. She had thoughts of applying for a job there once she earned her bachelor degree. Now that she knew all the people in human resource and a couple in other departments. That was one of the lessons being advised: utilizing the resources you have available when you are qualified.

All their stories had two things in common. They were planning their next step to success and staying away from conflicting people and conflicting situations. They also shared their opinion on how people get viewed once they get a criminal record. One part of their opinion was how people do not want to be involved with troubled people. They rather not get involved in anything that appeared disruptive to their lifestyle or livelihood. They would protect their happy and safe lives by ignoring all that threatened it. The second part was how a criminal record could not only affect getting a job but it could also affect friendships and possible relationships. All of them grew up in Newark and understood the adversities that were placed in children's paths to success. The adults at Newark City Hall have authentic concerns about their young summer hires. They encourage education and great life values. They make themselves available for the young workers concerns and their life's triumphs. They reminded them there were no stupid questions and to never stay in a situation that takes away all their options. They also reminded them of their choices and how people live by the decisions they make. She really enjoyed working there. It was like a life lesson class that she so desperately needed.

It was now the end of the summer, and she felt like she had another family at Newark City Hall. Hope said her goodbyes and began to prepare for college. She was looking forward to getting away from the projects and spending time with her girlfriends. She called them on their home phone and left messages with their family members for them to call her.

She advised them when she anticipated getting on campus so they could meet up and reminisce. She also wanted some advice on the college campus lifestyle and what it was like to have a roommate. She knew having a roommate would not be a challenge because she enjoyed people and planned to be flexible. She was eager to compromise. One of her challenges would be which clothes and accessories to take with her to school and which ones she would leave for her sisters to wear without her permission. She did not want to clutter her dorm's closet with all her belongings. She decided to take two weeks' worth of clothes and accessories and took her dad's advice and purchased a trunk and locked up her other clothes. Her dad lectured how her sisters liked to take their money and party then wear her clothes when they wanted to look cute. It would be fun to swap clothes with them, but her siblings clothes were too big for Hope, or not stylish enough. She stopped wearing their hand-me-downs clothes once she started working. Hope left a couple of items in the closet for her sisters to wear. She liked having something nice to wear when she wanted to go someplace special. If four people were constantly wearing the same inexpensive clothes, the life of the material lessened tremendously fast. When she got an invite to a social event that called for her to wear something casual, all her clothes have lint balls on them. That was very frustrating for Hope.

Once Hope got on campus, she was made aware that one of her girlfriends had dropped out and may be returning at a later date. Hope processed that information as college was socially and mentally difficult, but she did not get discouraged. She was determined to remain focused and complete the program in four years.

Hopeful Hope: Life Happens

College life was a different world with familiar people for Hope. She was happily living on campus. She was feeling inspired. She was confident that she would graduate in four years and would be able to obtain a job and finally escape the hood. She felt like she no longer lived in the projects. Although she was aware she must go home during the summer months, she felt like she had successfully escaped the hood! Spending time away from the projects was exactly what she needed right now. She had plans to enjoy it tremendously. She stared out of the window and appreciated the scenery. She noticed that there were no one sleeping on the ground, people relieving themselves, no fighting was going on, people were not arguing about a bunch of nothing, and the ground was clean! She noticed the green grass and the well-manicured bushes. The grounds consisted of crack-free walkways. The hallways smell of cleaning solution, and the walls were free of graffiti! She spent hours just walking around the campus by herself, enjoying the cleanness. The floors in the cafeteria looked as though one could eat off them. The cooks had on hairnets and plastic gloves. The recreation room was also clean. She could not believe her eyes! The carpet looked freshly vacuumed. Most of all, she enjoyed the fact that it was all parent-free!

Going to a college in New Jersey felt safe to her. She decided that it would be financially beneficial to attend a college in New Jersey. She felt physically and financially safe when she was near her family. She could always get a couple of dollars for food and travel if she needed it while she was attending college. The school was only one hour away from her home and her father's house. She did not own a car, but public transportation was available. Family and friends from the neighborhood with cars would transport her if she needed to get back and forth to school. They were supportive of the youths that were focused on college.

As Hope gave herself a grand tour of the college, she noticed some people she frequented at high school activities, fundraisers, games, and parties in Newark, Irvington East Orange, and Elizabeth. Everyone seemed to remember her name, but she only remembered their faces. She got plenty of invites to parties, school activities, and sororities. She hoped the parties were not violent because she would not attend them. She planned to do a little investigating before attending any parties. She would be asking many questions regarding the previous events. She refused to manage to get this close to her escape from the hood and then end up in jail for defending herself. She planned on living a long life. Being around people fighting and engaging in gun battles do not seems like a good ideal.

Today was Hope's first day attending college, and she felt so inspired. She did not have a neat or fancy hairdo. She did not have on her high heels or her fancy clothes. Her clothes were not completely color coordinating. She had on a pair of jeans and a pair of comfortable sandals. She had her hair pushed to the back with a hairband on. She was relaxed and optimistic about the challenges that were set before her. She thought nothing about being the first person in class. She thrived on being early. She had decided years ago to not conform to the stereotype of CPT (colored people time). That was a stigmatize that African-American people are frequently tardy.

This guy walked in the door and said, "Hey, Hope."

She looked up. She remembered his face from school but could not remember his name. He graduated years before her. She knew there was no way possible they could be in the same class. She was a freshman taking entry courses and he should be completing his last year of college. She verified the class with him to find that she was in the wrong class. Somehow she was turned around on her way to class. She really admired the green grass and healthy bushes. *The trees are so trees! It is amazing.* She felt like "Alice in Wonderland' when she was walking to class. Her and Tyrone began to laugh, and he walked her to the door and pointed her in the right direction. Before walking away, he gave her a brief description of the college and where the parties and activities are held. Then he gives Hope his number and invited her and her girlfriends to attend a party at Fairleigh Dickinson College. Hope thought her girlfriends would enjoy meeting more people and attending the party. She thought attending a party without the threats of guns and knife violence would be a nice change for all of them. Hope enjoyed partying, provided it was in a safe place.

Most of the freshmen went home for the weekend. Many lived less than ninety minutes from school. The cafeteria closes on the weekend, and if students do not have a car, getting cooked food can be a challenge. After the first month, Hope decided to go home. Her high school girlfriends went home every weekend. The bus schedule was abnormal on the weekend. The bus schedule was set for a bus to go to the college every two hours. The bus depot is a small building with a dirty bench outside. It has a dirty soda machine near the bench that does not work. Most students have a car or set up a ride before going home. Hope has no experience at weekend ventures. She assumed by the end of the weekend, she would catch up with her girlfriends and they would work something out. Her and her girlfriends went home Friday evening. The plan was to meet up Sunday, around noon, to head back to school. Friday night, they called Hope to invite her to a party. She declined because she wanted to spend time with her family. She loved the feeling of home. She just doesn't care for her home being in the projects. Saturday, her girlfriends called her again to invite her to another party. Hope declines again. After the party her girlfriends meets some guys who invites them out to dinner. After dinner they attend another party at the school. Sunday, Hope called her girlfriends' homes and their family members told her they went back to school. She called the hallway phone at school and got no answer. So she headed to the bus stop. There was a bus from downtown Newark that goes to downtown Paterson. There was no bus that goes from downtown Paterson to William Paterson College during the weekend.

When Hope got to the bus depot in Paterson, she called the hallway phones at school again, and still no one answered. She thought everyone were hungover from the party they attended the night before. She knew if she must walk, she had to begin soon. She did not want to walk up the hill in the dark. It would be getting dark in a couple of hours, and she wanted to be at the dorm before it gets dark. The path was a wooded area. The houses sat about a mile away from the street. There were no sideways to get college from the bus depot. You have to walk in the streets. It was a twenty-minute drive but a ninety-minute walk, and it was all uphill. Because it was all uphill, it could turn into a three-hour walk, especially when you are lugging bags. Hope began her walk in fear of getting stuck at the bus depot at night. She knew at some point her girlfriends would miss her. As she walked up the hill, her bags began to get heavy. Hope stopped and took a break. She was thirsty and had nothing to drink. She continued to walk and began thinking about funny jokes she was told to and funny situations she encountered. She kept herself entertained for most of her journey. She got to the college as it began to get dark. Her girlfriends were driving toward her. They called her house and Hope's mother told them she caught the bus after numerous attempts to contact them. They felt terrible. Hope was so happy to see them. That walk was long and scary. She had thoughts of animals jumping out of the woods and attacking her. Then an untamed men approaching her with crazy thoughts as he pretended to protect her from the animals. Cars were speeding pass her like they were trying to catch a last-minute gold sale. She could not remember ever being so scared. She vowed to never do that again. She would be sure to have a plan B the next time she decided to go home for the weekend.

Hope began meeting new friends during her weekend stay at college. She attended a party without her high school girlfriends. It was different being at a party without them. Her college friends were males and females. She really enjoyed being around them. The conversations were different, and they saw Hope differently. When she was with her high school girl-friends, she was constantly reminded about her high school conflicts or her family's bad decisions. Hope thought she could get used to being around people who did not focus on her too much. She just wanted to talk about life and other people. She no longer wanted to be the main focus of everyone's conversation. Sometimes she wondered if all this meant she was outgrowing her girlfriends, or if she needed to experience being around people that lived differently from her. After days of thinking about it, she believed she needed a change in her environment, and she was not outgrowing her friends. She knew that her and her friends would soon be venturing on in different directions in life. All of them would be meeting new friends soon.

Focusing on her class assignments became more difficult. She was constantly thinking about the dangers and confusions that awaited her at home. Although she was not there, her family continued to reside there. A couple of times during the school year, the school closed. Students had to seek counsel and justify their special need before they were allowed to remain on campus when it was closed. In fact, Hope felt like she might qualify as a special needs person who should be allowed to reside on campus when it was closed. She decided to go home during the school breaks. She began to reinvent her life's plan by planning the next five years of her life. Her original goal would remain the same, but she would rearrange many successes.

She no longer wanted to live with her siblings. She could not focus in her home regardless of the fact that she enjoyed being around her mother tremendously. She also enjoyed her siblings. However, everyone was grown and had moved on with their grown-up problems. Nobody seemed to laugh as much, and most of the conversations were regarding their problems. Hope assumed their problems existed because they resided in Newark. She believed that all their troubles would be resolved if they only move out of Newark. Her mother was always upset about her sibling's actions. When her mother was upset, she became upset. She felt her mother's pain. She often spoke to her mother about moving away from her adult siblings. Her mother took her parenting seriously and decided to stick around as long as she thought her children and grandchildren needed her. Hope thought she needed to get a job and move to a safer area, and hopefully, she would be able to focus on school.

She slowly began to fall behind in her class assignments. She knew as long as she believed, she would not achieve; it was a great chance that success was not hers. But she just could not be optimistic about her education right now. Her high school boyfriend began having financial worries at home and decided to drop out of college and get a job to help out his family. He began to visit Hope at college as if she needed yet another distraction. Despite the distraction, he kind of put things in perspective for her. He told Hope if she could not focus, she was just taking up space and wasting money. Someone else who was able to focus could be getting the financial aid and be achieving their goals in their lives. Hopeful Hope began to become hopeless again. She had to keep it real with herself and face reality. She had to tackle one issue at a time. She had to shit or get off the pot. She could get help to maintain her focus or give her seat to someone that will. Her desire to get a job and move out of the projects exceeded her desire to graduate from college. So Hopeful Hope dropped out of college with plans to return one day.

She woke up still on school campus. She had been focusing where she could live once she dropped out of college. She did not want to go back to the hood. She was not sure if she could stay with her boyfriend. Staying with her aunt and uncle meant a bunch of lectures. And everyone else had a full house, which meant sleeping on the floor out of a suitcase. She realized that her monthly menstrual was over a week late. She was irregular, but the pills made her regular. It would sometimes come early or last longer than normal when she was experiencing high-stressful situations. Dropping out of college qualified as a high-stressful situation. Thinking she could pray it away, Hope waited to see if her next monthly comes. It was now next month, and no menstrual. Her and her boyfriend went to the doctor, and it was confirmed that she was eight weeks pregnant. She had been consistently taking her birth control pills. One day, she became sick with the flu and decided to take some antibiotic pills. The antibiotic pills dissolved the birth control pills, and that was how she became pregnant while on birth control pill. So Hopeful Hope was back to feeling hopeless. She decided to go back home with her mother and create a five-year plan. Her mother was in the process of moving to another building in the projects. The building she now lives in had been condemned. She now had custody of Hope's nieces and nephews. Her mother expressed her disappointment in her. Then she began being short with her. She assumed her mother's disappointment would begin to escalate as the word about her pregnancy and dropping out of college began to circulate throughout the projects. Hope was now pregnant and was living back in the hood. Her boyfriend was standing by her side and was making sure she had all her necessities, including food.

Hope was on her way to the bathroom, and she felt wetness forming in her pants. She heard stories of how people's water breaks, but she was not sure if she was experiencing it. She just took a shower and thought maybe she did not dry herself completely. She realized where the wetness was coming from and perceived her baby might be on the way. She was now in panic mode and began dripping water throughout the house, looking for help. She became aware that she was home alone. She went back to the bathroom, cleaned herself up, put on a pad, grabbed her already packed bag, and headed down the block where her cousin, Danny, lived. His wife, Hazel, just happened to be looking out of the window and yelled, "Hope, is that you?" Hope looked at her and nodded. She did not want her to hear the fear in her voice. Then Hazel repeated herself, and Hope said, "Yes, Hazel, it is me."

It was now nighttime, and maybe Hazel did not see the nod. Then Hazel yelled, "Danny, get up. Hope is in labor, and she is very scared and is trying to be brave!" That made her smile. Fear was not an easy thing for her to conceal. She had never been good at pretending to be brave, although it was constantly taught in the hood to not show fear. Fear could get you picked on every day just for entertainment purposes. Danny did not have any plans to leave his home tonight, and he had been drinking. He took Hope to the hospital on the side roads, which had numerous potholes. Hope felt every bump but would not complain. He was her only means of transportation. She called her boyfriend before leaving the house and left word with his mother. He did not have a car. She kept telling herself, "We will be there any minute."

Finally, they arrived at the hospital. Always attempting to maintain positive thoughts in time of fear, she thought of her ride as labor practice. She constantly feared the process of having a baby. Every time she saw it on television, the mother was screaming, and nothing could seem to bring her comfort. Some women took their anger out on the baby's father. She kept practicing to remain calm. Once they filled out the hospital admission forms at the front desk, the doctor took her in. His examination proved that she was not dilated enough, and he suggested she go back home and come back in three hours. Hope refused to get back in the car with Danny because he had been drinking. She realized that he was not walking a straight line and was slurring his words. She was in such a rush when she first got in the car at the projects. She did not realize how tipsy he was. Danny had to go to work in the morning. He went home after talking the nurse to put Hope in a room. She assumed the nurse was well aware of the obvious.

Hope and her sister, Dina, was on their way home from the hospital with Hope's newborn. There was a new addition to the family! Many people requested the date and time of his birth date so they could play the numbers in the lottery. It was normal for a newborn's date of birth and time of arrival to be configured and played in the lottery in the hood. There have been many winners from that process. On their way home, her sister explained to her how she was now in the real world and how her life had become real. For the next couple of years, it would be all about her son's needs. She suggested that she took a moment and wrapped her head around how her decision to have a baby had spiraled her into adulthood at the age of nineteen. There would be no shopping, no clubbing, no hair salons, and no nail salons. Hope thought to herself, with all her planning and determination, she still ended up in the very place she planned to escape from. Life can be funny that way if you're not careful and extremely focus. She looked at her son and said, "Do not worry, baby, we will not be here for long. Mommy will figure out something." At that moment, she did not have a plan. She knew her determination would not allow her to settle for the hood life. She was determined to not raise her son in Newark.

Hope's mother continued to be short with her. Her disappointment in her leaving school was more overwhelming than she had imagined. Hope thought her and mother needed some time apart, so she moved in with her son's father, his two sisters, his mother, and her boyfriend. They made her feel welcomed and treated her like family. She felt so blessed to be living in a place that made her feel at home. His sisters looked at her like she was their big sister. They confided in her and shared their teenaged feelings. They asked Hope to take them shopping because they liked her taste in clothes. Hope sat in the kitchen when she was feeding her son while they helped their mother prepare meals. Hope shared with them how she became pregnant, although she was routinely taking her birth control pills. She learned from the people at Newark City Hall to share her learned lessons with other in similar situations. She enjoyed living with them.

Her son was now six months, and her boyfriend's family were moving to a smaller place. She moved back with her mom until her welfare benefits and apartment in the projects got approved. The disappointment in her mother's eyes was so painful she spent most of her time in her bedroom. She only left the room when she thinks her mother was in her room or had left the house. Hopeful Hope began to feel hopeless again. She began to think she would never get out of the hood.

She now has an income from welfare, and soon afterward, a one-bedroom apartment. Newark Housing Authority has a rule that a single parent with a child under two years old only qualifies for a one-bedroom apartment. Her and her son moved into their one-bedroom apartment without any furniture. Hope bought blankets and pillows, and they began to sleep on the floor. After a couple of welfare checks, Hope went to the local furniture store and layaway furniture. Soon, the apartment was fully furnished, with wall-to-wall carpet. She wanted to pretend she was in a better neighborhood when she steps into her apartment. She decorated her apartment the way the people on television who lives in the suburbs. She purchased some drapes for the windows and tiles for the floors. Fancy-looking picture hanged on the wall, and a small chandelier hanged in the middle of the living room. After walking pass all the crackheads, pissy hallway, and graffiti walls, she entered her suburban-like apartment. That was the only way Hopeful Hope could escape her sadness. She was more disappointed in herself than her mother could ever imagine. She remained hopeful as she constantly prayed to God for a sign of direction. As she waited for a sign, she knew she had to be proactive. She believed that God helps them who helps themselves.

Every Sunday, Hope began going to the corner store to purchase a newspaper to search for a job. The next-door neighbor noticed the paper in her hand and asked for the sports section. The elderly lady that sat out front asked for the obituary and advertisement. Soon, she was sharing her Sunday newspaper with her neighbors. They began to encourage her and offered to babysit when she went on a job interview. Today was a great day for Hope. She landed a job at a successful business. Her perseverance paid off like she knew it would. Hope's grandmother once told her, "Remaining optimistic is the key to success, and you can do whatever you believe you can do, but you must put the wok in. Dreaming any, praying is only half the battle." Hope had always lived her life by them words. After landing the job, she immediately began planning her escape out of the projects. First she purchased a car for transportation to and from work. Although she now makes enough money to move to a nice area, her self-confidence was holding her hostage. She thought she needed help, like a partner or a roommate. Her self-esteem was not high enough to move out of the hood by herself. She believed that she was not ready for the massive world, so she applied for a two-bedroom apartment in the projects because her son was getting older, and he needed his own bedroom.

A couple of months passed, and she was now moving into her two-bedroom apartment in the projects. It was bittersweet for Hope. She was happy for the extra bedroom, but she felt like the two bedroom might be a permanent fix. She joined the credit union to save money, so when an opportunity presents itself, she would be financially ready. She began to feel hopeless again. She thought no matter what she did, she would never get out of the projects.

The guy, she is dating, parents owned a two-family house. They were experiencing financial difficulties. He told Hope that one of their apartments were vacant and suggested they rent the apartment to help them out. He advised her that her part of the rent would be the same as the rent she was paying for the apartment in the projects. Although Hope had more than enough money saved for a plan B, she continued to feel safe living in the projects. Her rent was equivalent to one week of her pay. She did not have to pay gas and electric in the projects. She would have to pay gas and electric in the real world. She still thought that was an awesome idea. They were not asking for security. She did not have to do anything different. She would continue to pay the same amount of rent without going into her savings. In spite of her fears of the massive world, she was scared and knew she had to take advantage of this situation. She knew once she moved out, she would not be allowed back in because she now makes too much money to qualify for a subsidized apartment in the projects. After considering everything involved, she decided to move into that massive world. She saw this as a sign from God telling her that she was ready.

The house was in what Hope considered a middle-class neighborhood. The house was within blocks away from Baxter Terrance and other projects in Newark. The neighbor had gone bad since the sixties. Hope tried to make some improvements by painting the apartment and tiling the floors before moving in. She was determined to not live as the hood she knew. She also bombed the house for roaches. She noticed them when they did a walkthrough last week. His parents needed financial help, and Hope was raised to believe that we are all put on this earth to help each other. Hope's move was now twenty to thirty minutes, without traffic, away from her son's school. She used to live five to ten minutes away. She thought that was a small price to pay to get use to the massive world.

The sixth month's rents were now due, and her boyfriend neglected to pay his part of the rent. His mother asked Hope when do they plan on paying the other part of the rent. She advised Hope how her and her husband really needed the money. She was very nice and respectful, and Hope responded in a similar manner. It was now the second week into the sixth month and still no rent money from her boyfriend. He did not give a date when it would be available. After a couple of arguments, Hope paid the rent by herself, then she called her aunt and uncle and asked them if her and her son could stay with them until she could find another apartment. Her aunt and uncle welcomed her and her son into their home.

She moved all her belongings into the storage and moved in with them. It appeared that Hope was being forced into that massive world she tremen-dously feared. She knew her aunt and uncle were set in their ways. Living with them too long would be unsafe for everyone involved. Her aunt and uncle was a joy to live with. Hope's aunt enjoyed music and cooking. Sometimes she enjoyed them together. She introduced Hope to some of her recipes and the music from her era. She shared family stories and pictures that Hope did not know exist. Her uncles advised Hope about the upkeep on her new car. He enjoyed music and listening to his wife talk. Hope enjoyed living with them but did not want to overstay her welcome.

She had been living with her aunt and uncle for six months now. She managed to find a three-bedroom condo in Elizabeth. She thinks it would be a great idea to move her mother in with her and her son. Her mom refused because she had taken custody of her sister's children and she thinks it would be financially safer to stay in the projects with the children. The extra bedroom would also be great for when one of her siblings or nieces or nephews decided to spend a night. She smiled at the fact that she now had a guest room. She thinks to herself, *That is a suburban thing*. She never planned on that. Hope now felt like she was getting closer to her American dream, and she did it all by herself. It was a sensational feeling to finally escape the hood. Although it was not exactly a house in a middle-class area. She was out of the projects, and that's one step closer to her American dream. The condo was newly built. Her and her son was the first family to live in it. It was immaculate. Fresh paint, new tiles on the floor, new blinds on the window, new carpet in the bedrooms, new bathroom without mildew, and the best of all, no roaches! She had never lived in a place where there were no roaches. She no longer has a fear of the massive world. She thinks it has a lot to do with all the talks she had with her aunt and uncle while she was living with them. Her escape was not complete because she was a single parent and continued to go back to the projects so her family could babysit her son. He was attending a private school behind the projects. They helped her out by picking him up from school. Then he waited at her mother's house until she gets off work. It was a tough time in Hope's life because it's like she was still living there because she was there almost every day. She constantly fought the feelings of entrapment.

Hopeful Hope: Living the Dream

Hope was now beginning to meet friends at work. She was remaining hopeful in her new environment. They came from the same beginnings and similar triumphs. They traded telephone and pager numbers and began contacting each other after work. They enjoyed each other's conversations and began making plans to socialize after work. Tonight, they decided to go clubbing and enjoy the nightlife.

It was Friday night and was seventy degrees outside. They put on some jeans, a nice blouse, and some heels, and headed out for some laughs. After working and attending to their family all week, it was just what the doctor ordered. Jeans and a blouse was the normal dress code when they went clubbing. At the club, Hope's girlfriend, Ann, met a guy named Earl. He asked her to leave the club with him and go out to dinner. She did not feel comfortable going by herself. She asked Hope and the other girls to go with her. They all went to the club in one car. The guys went to the club in one car also. Hope and her girlfriends decided to leave the club and accompany the guys to dinner. As they followed the guys to the diner, they made up codes for when they were ready to leave or get feelings of being uncomfortable. Each of them left the diner with one of the guy's pager number. Hope left with Earnest's number.

Hope continued to persevere through life as she remained hopeful. She wanted to raise her son in a house, plus it was part of her American dream to be a homeowner. She did not think she could buy a house alone. She dreamed about owning her own home all the time. Almost everyone she knew that owned a home had a spouse or bought their home with someone. She continued to save her money so she would be prepared when the opportunity presents itself. She constantly initiated conversations with homeowners, conveying her desire to purchase a home. She thinks if she ever got an opportunity to purchase a house, she did not want to live in Essex County. She wanted to expand her horizons and reside in a different county. She was considering Union County. She enjoyed meeting new people and exploring different ways of living, listening to other people's mindsets, and witnessing other cultural ways.

Today was a great day for Hope. A friend of hers shared some uplifting news with her. She gave Hope a booklet about a low-income homeowner program. She thinks Hope would qualify for the program. She is a single parent with good credit. This is exactly what Hope had been praying for. She had been saving her money and paying her bills on time so she could be prepared when an opportunity presents itself. Now she has the money for a down payment. She had been paying her bills so her credit was good enough to get approved for financing. And she'd been saving her money so she could put down a large amount of money, making her mortgage afford-able. This program was being offered to low-income people. Hope could not believe her ears. She called the eight hundred number that was being advertised. The information was correct. She had to take a class to get a certification to buy a home. She had no idea such a program existed. Sharing her private thoughts and life plans had really paid off. Her friend may not have had known she was looking to purchase a home in Union County. Sometimes it was good to let people in and share your worries and struggles. Help could be sitting right beside you. The classes taught low-income people and first-time buyers the process of buying a home. It also educated the potential buy-ers about understanding the contracts regarding buy-ing and maintaining a new home. When she saw the word "*new*," she got so excited. Another roach-free home! A home that she and her son would be the first family to reside in. It will be awesome. Through the program, Hope was being offered an opportunity to purchase a newly-built townhouse in Vauxhall. It was love at first sight. She could not wait to move in her brand-new home. It was freshly painted, with new tiles on the kitchen floor, new carpet in the bedroom, new carpet on the stairs and living room, a one-car garage, and a patio. She was so excited. It also had one-and-a-half bathroom and a laundry room.

The signing was today, and Hope was so ner-vous. She kept changing her outfit. She had a bad habit of overdressing. She'd been keeping up with the latest fashion since she had been financially able to purchase her own new clothes. Finally, she got to the lawyer office and completed the signing. She walked out of the lawyer's office with a huge smile on her face. Once she got in her car, she began to sing all the way home. Hope began to sing the song that played at the beginning of a television show called *The Jefferson's*. The song goes, "Well, we movin' on up…to the east side… We finally got a piece of the pie." Then she began laughing.

Hope was now married to Earnest, with two children and a dog named Shabby.

They now resided in Vauxhall in the townhouse. Hope was now living her American dream. She went outside and sat on the bench of her front porch and began to cry. She thought back how she maneuvered through life to achieve her goal to escape the hood. She thought back at her life and wondered if she could have had did some things different regarding college. Maybe she could had commuted. The school was only one hour away, and the bus schedule was on point during the daytime. She thought maybe she could had scheduled her classes on two days, lessening the amount of days she would had been commuting. Some days she could had spent the night with one of her friends, making her process less stressful and less expensive. She had plenty of potential babysitters who might had supported her educational needs. She wondered if she tried hard enough. Maybe she gave up too easily. She had feelings of being incomplete.

Hope could not continue to ignore the void she felt regarding not completing college. She knew until she earns her bachelor degree, she would always feel incomplete.

Hope was off today. Her husband was at work, and her children were in school. She decided to go to Union County College and get some information regarding school. She was not sure if she should begin taking classes. She just wanted to check out the possibilities. She wanted to be home supporting her family and engaging in family fun. She wanted to be available to support and encourage her family, but she was unhappy and needed to fulfill that void inside her. She had concerns about how her unhappiness would affect her family. After going back and forth with her and her family's wants and needs, she decided to discuss it with her husband. He thinks it was a great idea and agreed to support her with the children and the household chores.

After being out of school for about fifteen years, Hope was on her way back to school.

Today was her first day of class. She was nervous and had thoughts of going back home. She sat in her car, in the school's parking lot, and began to pray. She asked for the strength to get through the day and the knowledge to know when to ask questions. All the students in her class was about half her age. Fortunate for her, she did not look her age. She constantly reminded herself that part of herself gratification depended on the completion of the class. The professor asked everyone to introduce themselves and tell the class a little something about themselves. Hope told people she's married with two children, and some of the students began to stare at her.

One student said, "Wow, you do not look old enough to have two children."

Hope said, "Yes, they are two and twelve years old."

Then another students said, "Wow! Really?"

Five weeks have passed, and Hope was in class. She was feeling comfortable. She had passed the first test with a B, and she had been handing in her assignments on time. Being in school was not affecting her household. She did her homework when everyone else was busy doing things they rather do without her or when they were asleep. They were having a class discussion, and Hope began to laugh. She caught the attention of the class clown. It made her thinks about her high school years. Her laugh always caught the attention of the class clown and began a relationship with a study partner or a friendly conversation in class. Smiles and laughter always softened the fear in her. When people laugh and smiles with her, she felt comfortable in her present space. It also signified the green light for her to begin a friendly conversation that always turned into laughter.

Hope woke up today to one of the most disturbing situations in her life. After numerous conversations with her husband, they decided to divorce. They attempted to keep it civil but arguments erupted, and Hope wished she could crawl in a closet and watch television. The thought of her children finding her in a closet watching television prevented her from doing so. She thinks back to how they met to reevaluate her decisions up to this point. Hoping she could learn from her past decisions in case she decided to go down that road again. Did they marry too young? Where they compatible? Where they ready to settle down? Did they even know what settling down meant? Was going back to school a good idea? Or was she being selfish at times? The transition forced Hope to drop out of school again. The stress was too much, plus she was being challenged with child care and finances. She moved far away from her family. Many of them do not own a car. Getting daily child care assistance from them was impossible. She could get weekend help. She really did not want to commute her children to Newark. The very place she struggled so hard to escape from. She preferred to go back there to only visit her mother. She did not want to subject her children to that environment no more than she had already. She thinks there had already been some irreversible damage already. Child care during the week was what she needed to continue to go to school. She managed to complete the semester with the help of her husband.

Now Hope was legally divorced. This result did not affect her American dream. As far as she was concerned, she had escaped the hood, and she would never go back. She was still in a good financial position. She had to scale back some by cutting back on fast foods and personal shopping. She also had to begin doing her own hair and manicures and pedicure. Hope decided to corn braid her hair and purchase nail care products to save money. As she grew tired of the corn braids, she would wear a fake ponytail or gel her hair back in a ponytail. As she managed to adjust to her new budget, she was saving plenty of money and maintaining her good credit score. She began getting her hair and nails done when she worked overtime. She continued to desire the need to increase her educational and personal growth. The void was still there, and it needed to be fulfilled. She began to create a five-year plan. She planned to complete her associate degree and moved to another town. The house her and her husband resided in has too many memories. One day, he went out drinking with his buddies and forgot he did not live there anymore. Hope never changed the locks because she knew he was not a threat. She woke up to him standing by the bed, watching her sleep. At first, she thought she was dreaming. He immediately became apologetic and left. Hope changed the locks on her next day off from work. Plus, Vauxhall was where his friends resided. She rather not run into them and constantly have unwanted conversations. She could no longer take the sad looks and that same old what-happened questions from his friends and acquaintances. With the challenges of child care, she decided to move closer to her job. She also needed a fresh start and thought it would also be good for her sons to meet new people. Her sons really wanted to stay in Vauxhall with their friends.

Hope now resided in Rahway and was dating Keith. She managed to purchase a one-family house. It was a colonial, with three bedrooms. The house was in Rahway, and she purchased it all by herself! She invited her family to her new home for dinner. Her mother stepped out of the car and looked at her house and began to smile. Hope began to cry. It gave her such joy to make her mother smile. She had achieved a great milestone in her life. She did it the traditional way. Without any programs or certification classes, she felt like she was in a great place in her life. She was physically fit, and her mindset was on point. She was feeling inspired about life and was living one of her American dreams. She lived closer to her job in Woodbridge, and her children have adjusted to their new schools. She had also found a good child-care program. One was being offered at the town YMCA. They also offered many activities her children could attend. Life was great. But she continued to feel that void and was determined to fulfill it. She decided to go back to school and completed her associate degree at Union County College.

After seven years of smiling, laughing, passing in assignments on time, studying for tests, and persevering, Hope has earned her associate degree in Computer System Information. She truly enjoyed attending Union County College. It had been a long time coming. Once the fear of going back to school ceased to exist and her concerns about being around people half her age, things began to flow smoothly. She cat walked across the stage with pride and great energy. She had a smile of appreciation. With her head held high, she accepted her image of a degree. The real degree got mailed out to the graduate's home. The students were previously advised of the school's process. She worked hard and made many sacrifices to earn her degree.

The day after graduation, Hope sat in her backyard and though about her accomplishments. She began to cry. She thought about her childhood friends who gave up and settled for a poverty lifestyle. She thought about the ones that had opportunities to improve their living condition and decided against it. The ones that turned to different substances to diminish their pain of failure and degrading experiences. They have grown content with their environment. It was look upon as a cultural thing by some. They view living in the hood less expensive. Regardless of the dangers that awaited them outside their doors, the low-quality education and low food quality at the neighbor's supermarkets, the cracked sidewalks that caused bad falls and broken heels, the pothole streets that caused additional car damage, they could just be themselves refusing to engage in personal growth. They learned from the streets, television, and from one another. To move out of the hood for some means pretending to be someone they are not. They thrived to be themselves with any excuse. Life was easy in the hood for some people that grew up there. Some people just refused to put the work in. There were some people that could live in poverty and be successful. They managed to avoid the dangers and lived under the radar. There were few and far in between.

It was now a couple of months after graduation, and there goes that feeling again. That feeling of a void. She had been going straight home from work—taking care of the house and kids, making happy memories and taking pictures for proof, spending quality family time, and planning yearly vacations. Yes, she has her associate degree, but the void was always for the bachelor degree. Because she waited fifteen years before returning back to school, she had to go the route of earning some credits in the community college first. Because she liked to finish what she started, she decided to graduate from UCC and not transfer once she achieved a 3.0 grade point average. She had a plan to substitute once she earned sixty credits. Then she realized with her work schedule and her home life it might not be doable at that time. She thinks maybe when the children get older. Hope decided to create another five-year plan. She had always been a planner because it kept her grounded. It gave her a feeling of existing and gives her things to thrive for. Without a plan, she felt like she was wandering through the day waiting for life to attack her.

Hope was on strike from her job and decided to check out Kean University's website. She had been considering going back to school. But she had concerns about her family's quality time. She had not applied or reviewed any information until today. The thought of going to a huge university made her nervous. She knew if she did not go back, she would forever live with regrets. She was getting closer to qualifying at her job for a full pension with benefits. She felt the need to plan her retirement more exactly. No matter her personal relationship, she wanted to be in a position to financially take care of herself. She knew relationships could deteriorate and end. She didn't think her marriage would end, and there she was, single with two children—being forced to figure things out by herself. She had always achieved her five-year plans that she had total control over. She had no plans of being divorced, but of course, that was out of her control. Looking back, she thinks they were not ready for marriage. They should had dated longer due to the fact they were in their twenties. Her retirement plans were to be an educator in elementary and high school. She had been talking to many elementary and high school teachers, and most of them appeared to be uninspired. She assumed talking to them would inspire her and present her with valuable information. They have worked through many changes in the educational system in New Jersey by the new governor. The teachers have feelings of no authority with their classroom lesson plans. They were being told to teach according to the governors' lesson plans. They were teaching the children to specifically pass a test. They were being evaluated according to how well the students process the test. Many life lessons have been taken out of the classroom according to the teachers Hope had been speaking to. She thinks it might be a good idea to not speak to them anymore, concerning teaching. She was getting concerned about her teaching plans, maybe a little discouraged. She was beginning to think maybe she should consider another retirement plan. Whatever it may be, she knew she must complete her bachelor's degree.

Today was Hope's first day at Kean University. She decided to take one class to get a feel of the processes. Kean University was much larger than Union County College. She got turned around on her first day and got a little discouraged. Everyone kept telling her that her class was right around the corner. She was so nervous she did not realize the signs were pointing straight toward the buildings. A smile came across her face once she realized the signs. She stood in the middle of the walkway and began to laugh. When she got to class, her professor told the class a story about how she got turned around when she was on campus. She had been teaching at Kean University for years, but there had been a lot of reconstruction, and some of the names on the buildings have been changed to honor people. She joked about how she got turned around also. No one understood why Hope found her story so funny. That story took away Hope's first day of class nervous condition. This time, Hope's laughter drew the attention of her professor. This was a change for her. Her professor was an elderly woman who volunteered at numerous animal shelters. She enjoyed telling stories, and Hope enjoyed listening to stories. She was a patient educator and encouraged Hope's writing skills. Hope knew she had room for improvement, which was why she was seeking personal growth. She praised her ideas and her desire to obtain her degree at her age.

In Hope's opinion, Kean University was a totally different institution than Union County College. The classes were less intense, and the professors were more available. The students were allowed more flexibility, and the classes seemed less complicated. Kean University had a dormitory. The students seemed to be in less of a rush and was more likely to assist another student with the class assignments. Hope was not sure if it was because they could walk home and not have the worries of traffic and the care of children, or if it was their relaxing dorm life they were enjoying. Hope felt more comfortable with the students at Kean.

It was now the third week of class, and Hope was feeling comfortable and inspired to take two classes the next semester. She had plans to go all year long. She would be attending winter, fall, spring, summer 1, and summer 2 classes. She wanted to feel complete and get rid of her void feelings as soon as possible. Because of some of the reconstruction, many classes were cancelled at short notice. The short notice made it difficult for her to get in another class, causing her graduation date to be pushed back. Hope attempted to make light of it by telling people she needed a break. Maxing out her tuition assistance that was being contributed from job also contributed to the delay of her graduation date.

Hope was now walking across the stage to collect a booklet her bachelor degree would be placed in. As she exited the stage, she immediately thought about her mother's disappointing looks when she decided to drop out of William Paterson College. It was unfortunate her mother was unable to witness this day. Unfortunately, she passed away before Hope could make her smile again. Seeing Hope, or a picture of her, walking across that stage would had caused her soul to smile. It would had given her bragging rights with her girlfriends. She always bragged about Hope's good grades and her desire to work. Hope was her only child that attended college immediately after high school. She was so proud when Hope received her acceptance letter. Her dad was unable to witness her great success also because he also passed away. Hope's dad made a point plenty of times that he knew she would be okay. Her dad would say, "Baby girl, you are destined for great things." He had never concerned himself about Hope because he understood her mindset. Her planning and desire to escape the hood reminded him of himself. Her father was one of her best friends. His lost touched her deeply.

As she sat in her basement, reminiscing about her Kean University years, tears rolled down her cheeks. Then she smiled at the fact that the void feeling was gone. She really had to get used to not feeling that way. She was really challenged this last semester. For the first time since she returned back to college, she registered for four classes. She was anxious to complete college and rid herself of that void feeling as she prepared herself for the next phase in her life. Her plan was to retire after working thirty years at the phone company and begin teaching. She had no control of the economy or the new president. She thinks she must be financially secured to leave a secure job with benefits. She needed a guaranteed teaching job before leaving a job that paid her a good salary. She did not want to be forced to move back to Newark, where she was guaranteed a cheap apartment. Where the danger awaited people outside their doors. Where the low food quality awaited the consumers at the local food markets. Where the smell of urine and feces greeted passersby as they stepped on the sidewalks.

During her last semester, she was advised of the master's program at Kean University. Earning a master's degree might qualify her a job as a college professor. Wow, she enjoyed the opportunities of having options. She decided to attend the seminar. She was impressed with the presentation and decided to apply. She submitted her application and received an email regarding her acceptance. Now that she had more information regarding the process of becoming a college professor, she needed to reevaluate her retirement plans. She would truly enjoy teaching poetry or creative writing. She enjoyed writing plays, books, and poems. She felt comfortable presenting her writings when she attended her creative writings and poetry class. Her first professor at Kean University really appreciated her creativity. She encouraged Hope to continue to write. That was the best advice she received from a professor. It was truly needed at that time. Hope was feeling a little discouraged upon her entry of Kean University. After Union County College, she considered Kean to be a huge place.

She now had three classes left to complete the master's program. She had once again maxed out her tuition assistance provided by her job. She had the option to wait until next year when she would be awarded another eight thousand for the year, or she could pay for her fall classes and attempt to graduate May 2018. She was no longer working overtime because she wanted to remain focused on her studies and get some rest when she didn't have to study. She was now registered for two classes. Although that void feeling was gone, she was still anxious to complete school. Hope had been attending school for about fifteen years, after not going for about fifteen years since attending college post high school. Some years she did not take a break by attending through the winter and summer sessions as she attended to her family. One of her plans were to begin living a home-work-free life. She wanted to begin to really enjoy her life without the worries of class assignments. She wanted to begin attending all of her family's functions and celebrations. She wanted to frequent musicals, plays, movie theaters, social gatherings, and parties. She wanted to visit islands, casinos, and go on a boat cruise at least once a year. She wanted to spend quality time with people who truly liked her and were capable of appreciating her desire to enjoy life!

I will like to dedicate this book to my parents. The sharing of their triumphs and life adventures have encouraged me to live my life without blame. It has given me the knowledge to persevere without considering my past upbrings. Their encouragement has truly been a blessing to me. I have learned from all their misfortunes, and I appreciate them for sharing their life stories with me.

Neighbors!!!

Growing up in apartment buildings was a lot of fun. It was exactly what I needed at the time. Constantly enjoying the interactions with people, developing and creating families and friends; a village of all sorts. People helping people physically, mentally, and socially and learning about people past endeavors, challenges, and triumphs. Sharing delicious recipes and how to cook the same dish multiple ways; and learning from people mistakes and their learned lessons. Getting what I will call "free counseling" from someone who may had or will experience similar situations. I truly enjoyed my neighbors when I lived in the apartments.

Then as I aged and had a family and children to raise, my needs and desires changed. I moved into a house. No one living on top of me or beneath me. There are now backyards, driveways, and alleyways separating me from my neighbors. Again, it is exactly what I needed at the time. A new neighborhood different people from around the world; a small melting pot. I was looking forward to meeting new people and learning about their country. My plan was to, constantly enjoy interacting with people. Plans on developing and creating families and friends; a village of all sorts. People helping people physically, mentally, and socially; learning about past endeavors, challenges, and triumphs. Sharing delicious recipes and how to cook the same dish multiple ways. Learning from people mistakes and their learned lessons. Getting what I will call "free counseling" from someone who may had or will experience similar situations, but it didn't quite work out that way. People are who they are and there is no changing how they view people, their situations, their beliefs, and their actions.

Now that I am divorced, retired, and single I have plenty of time on my hands. I enjoy writing and I have become more vigilant of my neighborhood. I desire the rural areas; where neighbors are at least a mile away,where interactions are planned and easily avoided, where I can sit in my backyard and read and write without any disturbance, where my neighbors don't have the luxury to ruin my day just because they can, where my neighbors creativity and construction to their house don't affect me in any way, where going food shopping becomes a nice road trip and relaxing outing,where I can walk in my back yard without the concerns of stepping in my neighbors' dog poop and where cats and dogs do not wander around freely.

Life is too short to have to constantly strategize my happiness around my neighbors insecurities. Some people are determined to choose their neighbors, regardless of the laws that are set in place. Communication and obtaining a common ground cease to exist for some. They are determined to have their way. Certain groups of people got it right when they created their own neighborhoods.

Conclusion

If these books can encourage anyone to live without blaming their past upbringings or their parents' actions, it will be a tribute to my legacy. I wrote these books to encourage children with similar beginnings as Hopeful Hope. We must be encouraged to persevere and know that success is a possibility. We must also share all our learned lessons with someone who has a similar upbringing. When someone plans their life, it can encourage the planner to maintain focus and lessen the possibility of an undesired detour. A planned life can result in a controlled happy life.

About the Author

Hope Baldwin is now enjoying her dream job as an adjunct professor at a community college. It was always her plan after retirement. She went to college part-time for around fifteen years while she was married, worked full-time, and raised her two sons. Hope's plans are to enjoy being an adjunct professor, spend as much time as she can with her granddaughter, and write books until her next retirement.